B
Q

WILL
SELF

A Story
for Europe

A
BLOOMSBURY
QUID

First published in Great Britain 1996

Copyright © 1996 by Will Self

The moral right of the author has been asserted

Bloomsbury Publishing Plc,
2 Soho Square, London W1V 6HB

A CIP catalogue record for this book
is available from the British Library

ISBN 0 7475 2897 7

Typeset by Hewer Text Composition Services, Edinburgh
Printed by St Edmundsbury Press, Suffolk
Jacket design by Jeff Fisher

'*Wir-wir*,' gurgled Humpy, pushing his little fingers into the bowl of spaghetti Miriam had just cooked for him. He lifted his hands up to his face and stared hard at the colloidal web of pasta and cheese. '*Wir müssen expandieren!*' he pronounced solemnly.

'Yes, darling, they *are* like worms, aren't they,' said the toddler's mother.

Humpy pursed his little lips and looked at her with his discomfiting bright blue eyes. Miriam held the gaze for a moment, willing herself to suffuse her own eyes with tenderness and affection. Blobs of melted cheese fell from Humpy's hands, but he seemed unconcerned. '*Masse!*' he crowed after some seconds.

'*Very* messy,' Miriam replied, hating the

testiness that infected her tone. She began dabbing at the plastic tray of his high chair, smearing the blobs of cheese and coiling the strayed strands of spaghetti into edible casts.

Humpy continued staring at the toy he'd made out of his tea.

'*Masse*,' he said again.

'Put it down, Humpy. Put it in the dish – *in the dish*!' Miriam felt the clutch on her control slipping.

Humpy's eyes widened still more – a typical prelude to tears. But he didn't cry, he threw the whole mess on the just-cleaned floor, and as he did so shouted, '*Massenfertigung!*' or some such gibberish.

Miriam burst into tears. Humpy calmly licked his fingers and appeared obscurely satisfied.

When Daniel got back from work an hour later, mother and son were still not reconciled. Humpy had struggled and fought and bitten his way through the rituals of pre-bedtime. Every item of

4

clothing that needed to be removed had had to be pulled off his resisting form; he made Miriam drag him protesting every inch of the ascent to the bathroom; and once in the bath he splashed and kicked so much that her blouse and bra were soaked through. Bathtime ended with both of them naked and steaming.

But Daniel saw none of this. He saw only his blue-eyed handsome boy, with his angelic brown curls framing his adorable, chubby face. He put his bag down by the hall table and gathered Humpy up in his arms. 'Have you been a good boy while Daddy was at the office – '

'You don't have an office!' snapped Miriam, who like Humpy was in Teri-towelling, but assumed in her case for reasons of necessity rather than comfort.

'Darling, darling . . . what's the matter?' Carrying the giggling Humpy, whose hands were entwined in his hair, Daniel advanced towards his wife.

5

'*Darlehen, hartes Darlehen,*' gurgled Humpy, seemingly mimicking his father.

'If you knew what a merry dance he's led me today, you wouldn't be *quite* so affectionate to the little bugger.' Miriam shrank away from Daniel's kiss. She was worried that, if she softened, let down her Humpy-guard at all, she might start to cry again.

Daniel sighed. 'It's just his age. *All* children go through a difficult phase at around two and a half; Humpy's no exception – '

'That may be so. But not all children are so aggressive. Honestly, Daniel, I swear you don't get to see the half of it. It's not as if I don't give him every ounce of love that I have to give; and he flings it back in my face, along with a lot of gibberish!' And with this Miriam did begin to cry, racking sobs which wrenched her narrow shoulders.

Daniel pulled Miriam to him and stroked her hair. Even Humpy seemed

distressed by this turn of events. '*Mutter*,'
he said wonderingly, '*Mutter*,' and
squirmed around in his father's arms, so
as to share in the family embrace.

'See,' said Daniel, 'of course he loves his
mother. Now you open a bottle of that
nice Chablis, and I'll put young Master
Humpy down for the night.'

Miriam blinked back her tears. 'I suppose you're right. You take him up then.'
She bestowed a glancing kiss on the top of
Humpy's head. Father and son disappeared
up the stairs. The last thing Miriam heard
before they rounded the half-landing was
more of Humpy's peculiar baby talk.
'*Mutter – Mutter – Muttergesellschaft*' was
what it sounded like. Miriam tried hard
to hear this as some expression of love
towards herself. Tried hard – but couldn't
manage it.

Daniel laid Humpy down in his cot.
'Who's a very sleepy boy then?' he asked.

Humpy looked up at him; his blue eyes
were still bright, untainted with fatigue.

'*Wende!*' said Humpy cheerily. '*Wende-Wende-Wende!*' He drew his knees up to his chest and kicked them out.

'Ye-es, that's right.' Daniel pulled the clutch of covers up over the bunched little boy. 'Wendy *will* be here to look after you in the morning, because it's Mummy's day to go to work, isn't it?' He leant down to kiss his son, marvelling – as ever – at the tight, intense feeling the flesh of his flesh provoked in him. 'Goodnight, little love.' He turned on the nightlight with its slow-moving carousel of leaping bunnies and clicked off the main light. As Daniel went back downstairs he could still hear Humpy gurgling to himself, '*Wende-Wende*,' contentedly.

But there was little content to be had at the Greens' oval scrubbed-pine kitchen table that evening. Miriam Green had stopped crying, but an atmosphere of fraught weepiness prevailed. 'Perhaps I'm too bloody old for this,' she said to Daniel, thumping a steaming casserole down so that flecks of onion, flageolets and juice spilled on to the table.' I nearly hit him today, Daniel, hit him!'

'You mustn't be so hard on yourself, Miriam. He is a handful – and you know that it's always the mother who gets the worst of it. Listen, as soon as this job is over I'll take some more time off – '

'Daniel, it isn't that that's the problem.'

And it wasn't, for Miriam Green couldn't complain about Daniel. He did far more childcare than most fathers, and certainly more than any father who was trying to get a landscape-gardening business going in the teeth of a recession. Nor was Miriam cut off from the world of work by her motherhood, the way so many women were, isolated then demeaned by their loss of status. She had insisted on continuing with her career as a journalist after Humphrey was born, although she had accepted a jobshare in order to spend two and a half days a week at home. Wendy, the part-time nanny who covered for Miriam during the rest of the week, was, quite simply, a treasure. Intelligent, efficient and as devoted to Humpy as he was to her.

No, when Miriam Green let fly the remark about being 'too old', her husband knew what it was that was really troubling her. It was the same thing that had troubled her throughout her pregnancy. The first trimester may have been freighted with nausea, the second characterised by a kind of skittish sexiness, and the third swelling to something resembling bulgy beatitude, but throughout it all Miriam Green had felt deeply uneasy. She had emphatically declined the amniocentesis offered by her doctor, although at forty-one the hexagonal chips were not quite stacked in her favour.

'I don't believe in tinkering with destiny,' she had told Daniel, who, although he had not said so, thought the more likely reason was that Miriam felt she had tinkered with destiny too much already, and that this would, in a mysterious way, be weighed in the balance against her. Daniel was sensitive to her feelings, and although they talked around the subject, neither of them ever came right out with it and voiced the awful fear that the baby Miriam was carrying might turn out to be *not quite right*.

In the event the birth was a pure joy – and a revelation. Miriam and Daniel had lingered at home for the first five hours of the labour, mindful of all the premature hospital-dashes their friends had made. When they eventually got to the hospital Miriam's cervix was eight centimetres dilated. It was too late for an epidural, or even pethidine. Humphrey was born exactly fifty-one minutes later, as Miriam squatted, bellowing, on what looked to Daniel suspiciously like a school gym mat.

One moment he was watching the sweating, distending bulk of his wife, her face pushed about by pain; the next he was holding a blue-red ball of howling new vitality. Humphrey was perfect in every way. He scored ten out of ten on the first assessment. His features were no more oriental than those of any other new-born Caucasian baby. Daniel held him tight, and uttered muttered prayers to the idea of a god that might have arranged things so perfectly.

The comfortable Victorian house in Muswell Hill the Greens called home had long since been tricked out with enough baby equipment to cope with sextuplets. The room designated as the young master's baby had had a mural of a rainforest painted on its walls by an artist friend, complete with myriad examples of biodiversity. The cot was from Heal's, the buggy by Silver Cross. There were no less than three back-up Milton sterilisers.

Daniel had worried that Miriam was becoming obsessive in the weeks preceding the birth, and after they brought Humpy home from the hospital he watched her closely for any signs of creeping depression, but none came. Humphrey thrived, putting on weight like a diminutive boxer preparing for life's title fight. Sometimes Daniel and Miriam worried that they doted on him too much, but mostly they both felt glad that they had waited to become parents, and that their experience and maturity was part of the reason their child seemed so pacific. He hardly ever cried, or was colicky. He even cut his first two teeth without any fuss. He was, Daniel pronounced, tossing Humpy up in the air while they all giggled, 'a mensch'.

Daniel and Miriam delighted in each stage of Humpy's development. Daniel took roll after roll of out-of-focus shots of his blue-eyed boy, and Miriam pasted them into scrapbooks, then drew elaborate decorative borders around them. Humpy's first backwards crawl, frontwards crawl, trembling step, unassisted bowel movement, all had their memento. But then, at around two, their son's smooth and steady path of development appeared to waver.

Humpy's giggles and gurgles had always been expressive. He was an infant ready to smile, and readier still to give voice. But at that time, when from many many readings of the relevant literature his parents knew he should be beginning to form recognisable words, starting to iterate correctly, Humpy changed. He still gave voice, but the 'Da-das' and 'Ma-mas' garbled in his little mouth; and were then augmented with more guttural gibberish.

Their friends didn't really seem to notice. As far as they were concerned it was just a toddler's rambunctious burbling, but both Daniel and Miriam grew worried. Miriam took Humpy to the family doctor, and then at her instigation to a specialist. Was there some hidden cleft in Humpy's palate? No, said the specialist, who examined Humpy thoroughly and soothingly. Everything was all right inside Humpy's mouth and larynx. Mrs Green really shouldn't be too anxious. Children develop in many diverse ways; if anything – and this wasn't the specialist's particular expertise, he was not a child psychologist – Humpy's scrambled take on the business of language acquisition was probably a sign of an exceptional burgeoning intellect.

Still, relations between mother and son did deteriorate. Miriam told Daniel that she felt Humpy was becoming strange to her. She found his tantrums increasingly hard to deal with. She asked Daniel again and again, 'Is it me? Is it that I'm not relating to him properly?' And again and again Daniel reassured her that it was 'just a stage'.

Sometimes, pushing Humpy around the Quadrant, on her way to the shops on Fortis Green Road, Miriam would pause and look out over the suburban sprawl of North London. In her alienation from her own child, the city of her birth was, she felt, becoming a foreign land. The barely buried anxieties about her age, and how this might be a factor in what was happening to Humpy, clawed their way through the sub-soil of her psyche.

Herr Doktor Martin Zweijärig, Deputy Director of the Venture Capital Research Department of Deutsche Bank, stood at the window of his office on the twentieth storey of the Bank's headquarters building looking out over the jumbled horizon of Frankfurt. All about him, the other concrete peaks of 'Mainhattan', the business and banking district, rose up to the lowering sky. Zweijärig's office window flowed around a corner of the Bank's building, and this, together with his elevated perspective, afforded him a view of the city cut up into vertical slices by the surrounding office blocks.

To his left, he could view an oblong of the university, and beyond it the suburb of Bockenheim; to his right the gleaming steel trapezoid of the Citibank building bisected the roof of the main station, and beyond it the old district of Sachsenhau-

sen. Zweijärig couldn't see the River
Main – but he knew it was there. And
straight in front of him the massive
eminence of the Messeturm, the highest
office building in Europe, blotted-out
most of the town centre, including,
thankfully, the mangled Modernism of
the Zweil shopping centre. Zweijärig
had once, idly, calculated that, if a
straight line were projected from his
office window, down past the right-hand
flank of the Messeturm at the level of the
fifteenth storey, it should meet the earth
two thousand and fifty-seven metres
further on, right in the middle of the
Goethehaus on Hirschgrab Strasse; forming a twanging, invisible chord, connect-
ing past and present, and perhaps future.

'We must expand!' The phrase with its
crude message of commercial triumphalism
kept running through Zweijärig's mind,
exhorting his inner ear. Why did Kleist
feel the need to state the obvious in quite
so noisy a fashion? And so early in the

morning? Zweijärig didn't resent Kleist's elevation above him in the hierarchy of the Venture Capital Division – it made sense. He was, after all, at fifty-five six years Zweijärig's junior; and even though they had both been with the Bank the same number of years, it was Kleist who had the urge, the drive, to push for expansion, to grapple with the elephantine bureaucracy the Treuhand had become and seek out new businesses in the East for the Bank to take an interest in.

But the rescheduling of the directors' meeting for 7.30 a.m., and the trotting-out of such tawdry pabulums! Why, this morning Kleist had even had the temerity to talk of mass marketing as the logical goal of the Division. 'The provision of seed capital, hard loans even, for what – on the surface – may appear to be ossified, redundant concerns, can be approached at a mass level. We need to get the information concerning the services we offer to the widest possible sector of the business community. If this entails a kind of mass marketing then so be it.'

Zweijärig sighed deeply. A dapper man, of medium height, with a dark, sensual face, he was as ever dressed in a formal, sober, three-piece suit. This was one Frau Doktor Zweijärig had bought at the English shop, Barries, on Goethestrasse. Zweijärig liked the cut of English business suits, and also their conservatism. Perhaps it was because he wasn't a native Frankurter, but rather a displaced Sudetenlander, that Zweijärig felt the brashness of his adoptive city so keenly. He sighed again, and pushed his spectacles up on his forehead, so that steel rims became enmeshed in wire-wool hair. With thumb and forefinger he massaged his eyes.

He felt airy today, insubstantial. Normally the detail of his work was so readily graspable that it provided his mind with more than enough traction, adhesion to the world. But for the past few days he had felt his will skittering about like a puck on an ice rink. He couldn't seem to hold on to any given thought for more than a few seconds.

Maybe it was a bug of some kind? His daughter, Astrid, had called the previous evening from Stuttgart and said that she definitely had a viral infection. She'd stayed with them at the weekend – perhaps that was it? Zweijärig couldn't remember feeling quite so unenthusiastic about work on a Tuesday morning. Or was it that Kleist's appointment had irked him more than he realised. Right now he would have rather been in the Klein-markthalle, buying sausage or pig's ears from Schreiber's; or else at home with Gertrud, pruning the roses on the lower terrace. He conjured up a vision of their house, its wooden walls and wide glass windows merging with the surrounding woodland. It was only twenty kilometres outside Frankfurt, on the north bank of the river, but a world away.

Zweijärig fondled the heavy fob of his car keys in the pocket of his trousers. He pushed the little nipple that opened the central locking on the Mercedes, imagining the car springing into life, rear lights flashing. He pictured it, under autopilot, backing, filling, then driving up from the underground car-park to sit by the kerb in front of the building, waiting to take him home.

'Childish,' he muttered aloud, 'bloody childish.'

'Herr Doktor?' said Frau Schelling, Zweijärig's secretary, who he hadn't realised had entered the room. 'Did you say something?'

'Nothing – it's nothing, Frau Schelling.' He summoned himself, turned from the window to confront her. 'Are those the files on Unterweig?'

'Yes, Herr Doktor. Would you like to go over them with me now?' Zweijärig thought he detected a note of exaggerated concern in her voice, caught up in the bucolic folds of her Swabian accent.

'No, no, that's all right. As long as the

details of the parent company are there as well – '

'Herr Doktor, I'm sorry to interrupt, but Unterweig has no parent company, if you recall. It was only properly incorporated in May of last year.'

'Incorporated? Oh yes, of course, how foolish of me. Please, Frau Schelling, I'm feeling a little faint. You wouldn't mind terribly getting me a glass of water from the cooler?'

'Of course not, Herr Doktor, of course not.'

She put the folder down on the desk and hustled out of the room. Really, thought Zweijärig, I must pull myself together – such weakness in front of Frau Schelling. He pulled out the heavy leather chair, the one he had inhabited for the past sixteen years, brought with him from the posting in Munich. He allowed the smell and feel of the thing to absorb him. He picked up the folders and tamped them into a neat oblong, then laid them down again, opened the cover of the first and began to read:

> Unterweig is a metal-working shop specialising in the manufacture of basic steel structures for children's playground equipment. The main plant is situated on the outskirts of Potsdam, and there is an office complex in the north-central district. As ever in these cases it is difficult to reach an effective calculation of capitalisation or turnover. Since May 1992, the shop has managed to achieve incorporation despite a 78 per cent fall in orders . . .

The words swam in front of Zweijärig's eyes. Why bother, he thought. I've read so many reports like this, considered so many investment opportunities, what can this one possibly have to offer that any of the others didn't? And why is it that we persist in this way with the Easterners? He grimaced, remembering that he himself had once been like the Easterners – no, not like them, worse off than them. There had been no one-to-one conversion rate for the little that the Russians had allowed him to take.

A thirteen-year-old boy carrying a canvas bag with some bread in it, a pair of socks and two books. One, the poems of Hölderlin, the other a textbook on calculus, with most of the pages loose in the binding. He could barely remember the long walk into exile any more. It seemed to belong to someone else's past, it was too lurid, too nasty, too brutal, too sad for the man he'd become. Flies gathering on a dead woman's tongue.

Had the fields really been that beautiful in Bohemia? He seemed to remember them that way. Smaller fields than those in the West, softer, and fringed by cherry trees always in bloom. It can't have been so. The cherry trees could only have blossomed for a couple of weeks each year, and yet that's what had stayed with him: the clutches of petals pushed and then burst by the wind, creating a warm, fragrant snowfall. He couldn't face meeting with Bocklin and Schiele at the Frankfurter Hof. He'd rather have a few glasses of stuff somewhere, loosen this damn tie . . . Zweijärig's hand went to his neck without him noticing, and shaking fingers tugged at the knot.

On her way back from the water-cooler Frau Schelling saw her boss's face half-framed by one of the glass panels siding his office. He looked, she thought, old, very old for a man of sixty-one. And in the past few days he seemed unable to concentrate on anything much. Herr Doktor Zweijärig, who was always the very epitome of correctness, of efficiency. She wondered whether he might have suffered a minor stroke. She had heard of such things happening – and the person concerned not even noticing, not even *being able* to notice; the part of the brain that should be doing such noticing suffused

with blood. It would be uncomfortable for
Frau Schelling to call Frau Doktor Zweijärig and voice her anxieties – but worse if
she did nothing. She entered the office
quietly and placed the glass of water by his
elbow, then silently footed out.

Miriam placed the feeding cup by Humpy's cot and paused for a moment looking
down at him. It was such a cliché to say
that children looked angelic when they
slept, and in Humpy's case it was meta-
phoric understatement. Humpy appeared
angelic when awake; asleep he was like a
cherry blossom lodged in the empyrean, a
fragment of the divinity. Miriam sighed
heavily and clawed a hank of her dark
corkscrew curls back from her brow.
She'd brought the feeding cup full of
apple juice in to forestall Humpy calling
for her immediately on awaking. He could
get out of his cot easily enough by himself,
but she knew he wouldn't until he'd
finished the juice.

Miriam silently footed out of Humpy's room. She just needed five more minutes to herself, to summon herself. It had been an agonised night on Humpy's account. Not that he'd kept Miriam and Daniel up personally – he never did that – but it had been a night of reckoning, of debating and of finally deciding that they should keep the appointment with the child psychologist that Dr Peppard had made for them for the following day.

Daniel had gone off to work just after dawn, giving the half-asleep Miriam a snuffly kiss on the back of her neck. 'I'll meet you at the clinic,' he said.

'You be there,' Miriam grunted in reply.

Dr Peppard had shared their misgivings about consulting the child psychologist, their worries that, even at two and a half, Humpy might apprehend the institutional atmosphere of the clinic and feel stigmatised, pathologised, mysteriously different to other toddlers. But more than that, she worried that the Greens were losing their grip on reality; she had seldom seen a happier, better-adjusted child than Humpy. Dr Peppard had great confidence in Philip Weston – he was as good at divining adult malaises as he was those of children. If anyone could help the Greens to deal with their overweening affection for their child – which Dr Peppard thought privately was the beginning of an extreme, hot-housing tendency – then it would be Philip Weston.

Miriam now lay, face crushed into pillow, one ear registering the *Today Programme* – John Humphreys withering at some junior commissioner in Brussels – the other cocked for Humpy's awakening, his juice-slurping, his agglutinative wake-Miriam-up call.

This came soon enough. '*Bemess-bemess-bemess – !*' he cried, shaking the side of his cot so that it squeaked and creaked. '*Bemessungsgrundlage,*' he garbled.

'All right, Humpy,' Miriam called out to him. 'All right, Humpy love, I'm coming!' then buried her head still further in the pillow. But she couldn't shut it out: '*Bemess-bemess-bemessungsgrundlage!*' Better to get up and deal with him.

An hour or so later Miriam was sitting at her dressing table, which was set in the bay window of the master bedroom, with Humpy on her lap. It was a beautiful morning in late spring and the Greens' garden – which Daniel lavished all of his professional skills on – was an artfully disordered riot of verdancy. Miriam sighed, pulling the squirming Humpy to her breast. Life could be so sweet, so good; perhaps Dr Peppard was right and she was needlessly anxious about Humpy. 'I *do* love you so much, Humpy – you're my favourite boy.' She kissed the soft bunch of curls atop his sweet head.

Humpy struggled in her embrace and reached out to one of the bottles on the dressing table. Miriam picked it up and pressed it into his fat little palm. 'This is kohl, Humpy – can you say that, "kohl"? Try to.'

Humpy looked at the vial of make-up intently; his small frame felt tense in Miriam's arms. '*Kohl*,' he said. '*Kohl!*' he reiterated with more emphasis.

Miriam broke into peals of laughter. 'That's a clever Humpy!' She stood up, feeling the curious coiled heft of the child as she pulled him up with her. She waltzed Humpy a few steps around the room.

'*Kohl!*' he cried out merrily, and mother and son giggled and whirled; and would have gone on giggling and whirling were it not for the sound of the front door bell.

'Bugger!' said Miriam, stopping the dance. 'That'll be the postman, we'd better go and see what he wants.'

The change in Humpy was instantaneous – almost frighteningly so. '*Pohl!*' he squealed. '*Pohl–Pohl–Pohl!*' and then all his limbs flew out, his foot catching Miriam in her lower abdomen.

She nearly dropped him. The moment before, the moment of apparently mutual comprehension was gone, and in its place

30

was a grizzling gulf. 'Oh Humpy – please, Humpy!' Miriam struggled to control his flailing arms. 'It's OK, it's OK,' she soothed him, but really it was she who needed the soothing.

Philip Weston entered the waiting room of the Gruton Child Guidance Clinic moving silently on the balls of his feet. He was a large, adipose man, who wore baggy corduroy trousers to disguise his thick legs and bulky arse. Like many very big men he had an air of stillness and poise about him. His moon face was cratered with jolly dimples, and his bright-orange hair stood up in a cartoon flammable ruff. He was an extremely competent clinician, with an ability to build a rapport with even the most disturbed children.

The scene that met his forensically attuned eyes was pacific. The Green family were relaxed in the bright sunny waiting room. Miriam sat leafing through a magazine, Daniel sat by her, working away at the occupational dirt beneath his nails, using the marlinespike on his clasp knife. At their feet was Humpy. Humpy had, with Daniel's assistance, in the fifteen minutes since they'd arrived at the clinic, managed to build a fairly extensive network of Brio toy-train tracks, incorporating a swing bridge and a level crossing. Of his own accord he had also connected up a train, some fifteen cars long, and this he was pushing along with great finesse, making the appropriate 'Woo-woo' noises.

'I'm Philip Weston,' said the child psychologist. 'You must be Miriam and Daniel, and this is – ?'

'Humpy – I mean Humphrey.' Miriam Green lurched to her feet, edgy at once.

'Please.' Philip damped her down, and knelt down himself by the little boy. 'Hello, Humpy, how are you today?'

Humpy left off mass-transportation activities and looked quizzically at the clownish man, his sharp blue eyes meeting

Philip's waterier gaze. '*Besser*,' he said at length.

'Better?' queried Philip, mystified.

'*Besser*,' Humpy said again, with solemn emphasis. '*Besserwessi!*' and as if this gobbledygook settled the matter, he turned back to the Brio.

Philip Weston regained the foundation of his big legs. 'Shall we go in,' he said to the Greens, and indicated the open door of his consulting room.

Neither Miriam nor Daniel had had any idea of what to expect from this encounter, but in the event they were utterly charmed by Philip Weston. His consulting room was more in the manner of a bright, jolly nursery, a logical extension of the waiting room outside. While Humpy toddled about, picking up toys from plastic crates, or pulling down picture books from the shelves, the child psychologist chatted with his parents. So engaging and informal was his manner that neither Miriam nor Daniel felt they were being interviewed or assessed in any way – although that was, in fact, what was happening.

Philip Weston chatted their worries out of them. His manner was so relaxed, his demeanour so unjudgmental, that they both felt able to voice their most chilling fears. Was Humpy perhaps autistic? Or brain-damaged? Was Miriam's age in some way responsible for his learning difficulty? To all of these Philip Weston was able to provide instant and total refutation. 'You can certainly set your-selves at rest as far as any autism is con-cerned,' he told them. 'Humpy engages emotionally and sympathetically with the external world; as you can see now, he's using that stuffed toy to effect a persona-tion. No autistic child ever engages in such role-playing activity.'

Nor, according to Philip, was Humpy in any way retarded: 'He's using two or more coloured pencils in that drawing, and he's already forming recognisable shapes. I think I can tell you with some authority that, if anything, this represents advanced, rather than retarded, ability for a child of his age. If there is a real problem here, Mr and Mrs Green, I suspect it may be to do with a gift rather than a deficiency.'

After twenty minutes or so of chatting and quietly observing Humpy, who continued to make use of Philip Weston's superb collection of toys and diversions, the child psychologist turned his attention directly to him. He picked up a small tray full of outsized marbles from his desk and called to the toddler, 'Humpy, come and look at these.' Humpy came jogging across the room, smiling broadly. In his cute, Osh-Kosh bib 'n' braces, his brown curls framing his chubby face, he looked a picture of health and radiance.

Philip Weston selected one of the marbles and gave it to Humpy. 'Now, Humpy,' he said, 'if I give you two of these marbles' – he rattled the tray – 'will you give me that marble back?' Without even needing to give this exchange any thought Humpy thrust the first marble in the child psychologist's face. Philip took it, put it in the tray, selected two other shiny marbles and gave them to him. Humpy grinned broadly. Philip turned to Miriam and Daniel saying, 'This is really quite exceptional comprehension for a child Humpy's age – ' He turned back to Humpy.

'Now, Humpy, if I give you two of these remaining marbles, will you give me those two marbles back?'

Humpy stared at Philip for some seconds, while storm clouds gathered in his blue, blue eyes. The little boy's brow furrowed, and his fist closed tightly around his two marbles. '*Besserwessi!*' he spat at Philip, and then, '*Grundgesetz!*'.

It was to Philip's credit, and a fantastic exemplar of his clinical skills, that he didn't react at all adversely to these bits of high-pitched nonsense, but merely put the question again: 'These two marbles, Humpy, for your two, what do you say?'

Humpy opened his hand and looked at

the two blue marbles he had in his possession. Philip selected two equally shiny blue marbles from the tray and proffered them. There was silence for some moments while the two parties eyed one another's merchandise. Then Humpy summoned himself. He put one marble very carefully in the side pocket of his overalls, and the other in the bib pocket. This accomplished, he said to Philip with great seriousness, '*Finanzausgleichgesetz*,' turned neatly on his heels, and went back to the scribbling he'd been doing before the child psychologist called him over.

Daniel Green sighed heavily, and passed a hand through his hair. 'Well, now you've seen it, Philip – that's the Humpy we deal with most of the time. He talks this . . . this . . . I know I shouldn't say it, but it's gibberish, isn't it?'

'Hmmm . . .' Philip was clearly giving the matter some thought before replying. 'We-ell, I agree, it doesn't sound like anything recognisably meaningful, but there is definitely something going on here, Humpy is communicating *something*, something that he thinks we might comprehend. There's great deliberation in what he's saying . . . I don't know, I don't know . . .' He shook his head.

'What?' Miriam was sitting forward on the edge of her chair; she was trying to remain calm, but her troubled expression betrayed her. 'What do you think? Please, don't hold anything back from us.'

'It could be pure speculation. It's something I've never seen before. I tell you, if I didn't know any better I'd be prepared to hazard the idea that young Humpy was originating some kind of idiolect, you know, a private language. His cognitive skills are, as I said, quite remarkably developed for his age. If you don't mind, I'd like to get a second opinion here.'

'What would that entail?' asked Miriam. She was clearly appalled by this turn of events, but Daniel, by contrast, was leaning forward, engaged, intrigued.

'Well, it just so happens that we have a Dr Grauerholtz visiting us here at the Gruton at the moment. This is a marvellous opportunity. He's a former director of the clinic, now based at the Bettelheim Institute in Chicago, *and* he's without doubt the foremost expert on human-language acquisition in either Europe or the USA. If he's available I'd like him to pop in right away and have a chat with Humpy as well. See if we can get to the bottom of this young man's verbal antics. What do you say?'

'What is the basis of assessment?'
  'The same as it's always been.'
  'Meaning . . .?'
  'Meaning that they did have an open order book, that they did have a capital fund – of some sort. Meaning that both have been subject to the one-on-one conversion rate, and those monies remain in escrow. Meaning that precisely, Herr Doktor.'

'Yes, yes, of course, I know all of that. I know all of that.'

It was late in the morning and Zweijärig was feeling no better – perhaps worse. He'd groped his way through the Unter-weig file and now was attempting to discuss its contents with Hassell, his capitalisation expert. At least he'd taken the leap and got Frau Schelling to cancel the meeting with Bocklin and Schiele. 'The unheard-of must be spoken.'

'I'm sorry, Herr Doktor?' Hassell was looking curiously at his boss. Zweijärig noted, inconsequentially, how pink Hassell's forehead was. Pink fading to white at the hairline, just like a slice of ham.

'Ah, um, well . . .' I spoke aloud? Zweijärig fumbled the ball of thought. What is this – am I really losing my marbles? 'I mean to say, the conversion rate, Hassell, it remains as stupid today as when Kohl proposed it. It's wrecked our chances of building the economy the way we might wish to. It doesn't reflect the constitution – such as it was; and it doesn't accord with the law governing redistribution of fiscal apportionments to the Länder.'

Hassell was staring hard at Zweijärig during this speech. It was about the closest he could remember his boss getting to discussing politics directly in the four years they'd worked together. He normally skated around such topics, avoiding them with something approaching flippancy. Hassell steepled his plump fingers on the edge of the desk, pursed his plump lips, and ventured a query. 'So, Herr Doktor, would you have favoured Pohl's proposal? Do you think things would have gone that much smoother?'

'Pohl-Kohl. Kohl-Pohl. It hardly matters which bloody joker we have sitting on top of the Reichstag. We're a nation of displaced people, Herr Hassell. We're displaced from our past, we're displaced from our land, we're displaced from each other. That's the European ideal for you, eh – we're closer to people in Marseilles or Manchester than we are to those in Magdeburg. It's an ideal of mass society rather than homeland, ach!'

Zweijärig was, Hassell noted, breathing heavily, panting almost. His tie was loosened, the top button of his shirt undone. Hassell didn't wish to be intrusive, but he ought really to enquire. 'Are you feeling all right, Herr Doktor?'

'All right, yes, yes, Herr Hassell, I feel all right. I feel like the smart-aleck Westerner I've become, eh? Wouldn't you say?'

'It's not my position, Herr Doktor – '

'No, no, of course not, of course not. It's not your position. I'm sorry, Herr Hassell, I'm not myself today, I'm like Job on his dungheap – you know that one, d'you? It's in the Stadel, you should go and look at it. *Job on his Dungheap*. Except in *our* case the dungheap is built of glass and steel, hmm?'

'Dungheap, Herr Doktor?' said Hassell, trying to look unobtrusively over his shoulder, trying to see whether Frau Schelling was in the outer office.

'Playing with shit, Herr Hassell, playing with shit. Have you ever heard the expression that money *is* shit, Herr Hassell?'

'Herr Doktor?'

'Money *is* shit. No, well, I suppose not. Y'know, there are ghosts here in Frankfurt, Herr Hassell, you can see them if you squint. You can see them walking about – the ghosts of the past. This city is built on money, so they say. Perhaps it's built on shit too, hmm?'

And with this gnomic – if not crazy – remark, Herr Doktor Martin Zweijärig stood up, passed a sweaty hand across his brow, and made for the door of his office, calling over his shoulder, 'I'm going for a glass of stuff, Herr Hassell. If you would be so good, please tell Frau Schelling I'll be back in a couple of hours.' Then he was gone.

Hassell sighed heavily. The old man was unwell, disturbed even. He was clearly disoriented; perhaps Hassell should stop him leaving the bank building? Ethics and propriety did battle in the arid processes of Hassell's mind for some seconds, until ethics won – narrowly.

Hassell got up and quit the office at a near-jog, the bunches of fat above his broad hips jigging like panniers on a donkey. But when he reached the lifts Zweijärig had gone. He turned back to the office and met Frau Schelling. 'The Deputy Direktor, Frau Schelling, do you think – ?'

'I think he's ill, Herr Hassell – he's behaving very oddly. I called Frau Doktor Zweijärig just now. I hated going behind his back like that, but – '

'You did the right thing, Frau Schelling. What did Frau Doktor Zweijärig say?'

'Oh, she's noticed it as well. She's driving into town right now. She says she'll be here within the hour. But where has he gone?'

'He said something about getting a glass

of stuff. Do you think he's gone to Sachsenhausen?'

'I doubt it, he can't stand the GIs there. No, there's a tavern near the station he often goes to. I'll bet he's gone there now.' Frau Schelling shook her head sorrowfully. 'Poor man, I do hope he's all right.'

'Miriam and Daniel Green, this is Dr Grauerholtz . . . and this is Humpy.' Philip Weston stood in the middle of his consulting room making the introductions. Dr Grauerholtz was a tiny little egg of a man, bald, bifocaled, and wearing a quite electric blue suit. The contrast between the two psychologists was straightforwardly comic, and despite the seriousness of the situation, Daniel and Miriam exchanged surreptitious grins and jointly raised their eyebrows.

'Hello,' said Dr Grauerholtz warmly. He had a thick but not unpleasant German accent. 'Philip tells me that we have a most unusual young fellow with us today – you must be very proud of him.'

'Proud?' Miriam Green was becoming agitated again. Dr Grauerholtz and Philip Weston exchanged meaningful glances. Dr Grauerholtz indicated that they should all sit down. Then, with rapid, jerky movements he stripped off his funny blue jacket, threw it over a chair, reversed the chair, and sat down on it facing them with his elbows crossed on the back.

'I don't think I will be in any way upsetting you, Mr and Mrs Green, if I tell you that my colleague has managed to do a rudimentary Stanford-Binet test on Master Humpy – '

'Stanford-Binet?' Miriam was becoming querulous.

'I'm sorry, so-called intelligence test. Obviously such things are very speculative with such a young child, but we suspect that Humpy's IQ may be well up in the hundred and sixties. He is, we believe, an exceptionally bright young fellow. Now, if you don't mind . . .'

Dr Grauerholtz dropped backwards off the chair on to his knees and then crawled towards Humpy across the expanse of carpet. Humpy, who had payed no attention to Dr Grauerholtz's arrival, was playing with some building blocks in the corner of the room. He had managed to construct a sort of pyramid, or ziggurat, the top of which was level with the first shelf of a bookcase, and now he was running toy cars up the side of this edifice and parking them neatly by the spines of the books.

'That's a good castle you've got there, Humpy,' said Dr Grauerholtz. 'Do you like castles?'

Humpy stopped what he was doing and regarded the semi-recumbent world authority on human-language acquisition with an expression that would have been called contemptuous in an older individual. '*Grundausbildung!*' he piped, scooting one of the toy cars along the shelf. Dr Grauerholtz appeared rather taken aback,

and sat back on his heels. Daniel and
Miriam gave each other weary looks.

'*Grundausbildung?*' Dr Grauerholtz re-
peated the gibberish with an interrogative-
sounding swoop at the end. Humpy
stopped what he was doing, tensed, and
turned to give the doctor his full attention.
'*Ja,*' he said after a few moments, '*grundausbildung.*'

'*Grundausbildung für . . .?*' gargled the
doctor.

'*Für bankkreise,*' Humpy replied, and
smiled broadly.

The doctor scratched the few remaining
hairs on his head, before saying, 'Humpy,
verstehen sie Deutsch?'

'*Ja,*' Humpy came back, and giggled.
'*Geschäft Deutsch.*' Then he resumed playing with the toy car, as if none of this
bizarre exchange were of any account.

Dr Grauerholtz stood up and came back
to where the adults were sitting. They
were all staring at him with frank astonish-
ment, none more so than Miriam Green.

To look at her you might have thought she was in the presence of some prophet, or messiah. 'Doc-Doctor Grau-Grauerholtz,' she stuttered, 'c-can you understand what Humpy is saying?'

'Oh yes,' the Doctor replied. He was now grinning as widely as Humpy. 'Quite well, I think. You see, your son is speaking . . . How can I put it? He's speaking what you would call "business German".'

' "Business German"?' queried Philip Weston. 'Isn't that a bit unusual for an English child of two and a half?'

Dr Grauerholtz had taken his bifocals off and was cleaning them with a small soft cloth that he'd taken from his trouser pocket. He looked at the three faces that gawped at him with watery, myopic eyes, and then said, 'Yes, yes, I suppose a bit unusual, but hardly a handicap.' He smiled, a small wry smile. 'Some people might say it was a great asset – especially in today's European situation, yes?'

Humpy chose that moment to push

over the pyramid of building blocks he'd made. They fell with a delightful local crash; and Humpy began to laugh. It was the happy, secure laugh of a well-loved child – if a tad on the guttural side.

They found Herr Doktor Martin Zweijärig sitting on the pavement outside the station. His suit was scuffed-about and dirty, his face was sweaty and contorted. All around him the human flotsam roiled: Turkish guest workers, junkies, asylum-seekers and tourists. There was hardly an ethnic German to be found in this seedy quarter of the European financial capital. Zweijärig was conscious, but barely so. The stroke had robbed him of his strength – he was as weak as a two-year-old child; and quite naturally – he was talking gibberish.

A NOTE ON THE AUTHOR

Will Self is the author of five books. His first collection of stories was *The Quantity Theory of Insanity*. His most recent collection of short stories is *Grey Area*. His new novel *Great Apes* will be published in 1997. He lives in London.

Margaret Atwood	*The Labrador Fiasco*
T. Coraghessan Boyle	*She Wasn't Soft*
Nadine Gordimer	*Harald, Claudia, and their Son Duncan*
David Guterson	*The Drowned Son*
Jay McInerney	*The Queen and I*
Candia McWilliam	*Change of Use*
Patrick Süskind	*Maître Mussard's Bequest*
Joanna Trollope	*Faith*
Tobias Wolff	*Two Boys and a Girl*

AVAILABLE AS BLOOMSBURY CLASSICS

Surfacing, Margaret Atwood
Wilderness Tips, Margaret Atwood
The Snow Queen and Other Fairy Stories,
    Hans Christian Andersen
At The Jerusalem, Paul Bailey
Old Soldiers, Paul Bailey
Flaubert's Parrot, Julian Barnes
Ten, A Bloomsbury Tenth Anniversary Anthology
The Piano, Jane Campion and Kate Pullinger
The Passion of New Eve, Angela Carter
Emperor of the Air, Ethan Canin
Alice's Adventures in Wonderland, Lewis Carroll
A Christmas Carol, Charles Dickens
Poor Cow, Nell Dunn
The Lover, Marguerite Duras
The Birds of the Air, Alice Thomas Ellis
The Virgin Suicides, Jeffrey Eugenides
Utopia and Other Places, Richard Eyre
The Great Gatsby, F. Scott Fitzgerald
Bad Girls, Mary Flanagan
The Lagoon and Other Stories, Janet Frame
Mona Minim, Janet Frame
Owls Do Cry, Janet Frame
Across the Bridge, Mavis Gallant
Green Water, Green Sky, Mavis Gallant
Something Out There, Nadine Gordimer
Christmas Stories, Selected by Giles Gordon
Ghost Stories, Selected by Giles Gordon
Carol, Patricia Highsmith
The 158-Pound Marriage, John Irving
Setting Free the Bears, John Irving
Trying to Save Piggy Sneed, John Irving

Jimmy and the Desperate Woman, D. H. Lawrence
Einstein's Dreams, Alan Lightman
Bright Lights, Big City, Jay McInerney
Debatable Land, Candia McWilliam
Bliss and Other Stories, Katherine Mansfield
The Garden Party and Other Stories, Katherine Mansfield
So Far from God, Patrick Marnham
Lies of Silence, Brian Moore
The Lonely Passion of Judith Hearne, Brian Moore
The Pumpkin Eater, Penelope Mortimer
Lives of Girls and Women, Alice Munro
The Country Girls, Edna O'Brien
Coming Through Slaughter, Michael Ondaatje
The English Patient, Michael Ondaatje
In the Skin of a Lion, Michael Ondaatje
Running in the Family, Michael Ondaatje
Let Them Call it Jazz, Jean Rhys
Wide Sargasso Sea, Jean Rhys
Keepers of the House, Lisa St Aubin de Téran
The Quantity Theory of Insanity, Will Self
The Pigeon, Patrick Süskind
The Heather Blazing, Colm Tóibín
Cocktails at Doney's and Other Stories, William Trevor
The Choir, Joanna Trollope
Angel, All Innocence, Fay Weldon
Oranges are not the only fruit, Jeanette Winterson
The Passion, Jeanette Winterson
Sexing the Cherry, Jeanette Winterson
In Pharaoh's Army, Tobias Wolff
This Boy's Life, Tobias Wolff
Orlando, Virginia Woolf
A Room of One's Own, Virginia Woolf